Squeak's Good Idea

Words by Max Eilenberg

Pictures by Patrick Benson

WALKER BOOKS
AND SUBSIDIARIES
LONDON • BOSTON • SYDNEY

Squeak's
Good Idea

For Tom and Danny
M.E.

For Alexander Agnew
P.B.

First published 2001 by Walker Books Ltd
87 Vauxhall Walk, London SE11 5HJ

10 9 8 7 6 5 4 3 2 1

Text © 2001 Max Eilenberg
Illustrations © 2001 Patrick Benson

This book has been typeset in Minion Condensed

Printed in Italy

British Library Cataloguing in Publication Data:
a catalogue record for this book
is available from the British Library

ISBN 0-7445-7507-9

"I've got a good idea," said Squeak.

"Let's all go out. Who wants to come?"

"I'm a bit busy," said Poppa.

Momma and Tumble were busy too.

"Oh," said Squeak.

"Then I'll have

to go on my own."

He opened the door
and looked out.
"Hmm," he said.
"It might be cold."

So he went to the cupboard
and fetched his coat.

And then, just to be on the safe
side, he got his mittens, his hat
and his warmest trousers as well.

"Momma," he called.

"Can I borrow your scarf?"

"Of course you can,"
said Momma.

Squeak went back to the door.

He looked out.

"Hmm," he said.

"It might rain."

So he went to the hall and fetched his mac. And then, just to be on the safe side, he got his wellington boots and some extra socks as well.

"Poppa," he called. "Can I borrow your umbrella?"

"Of course you can," said Poppa.

Squeak went back to the door.

He looked out.

"Hmm," he said.

"I might get hungry."

So he went to the kitchen
and fetched some biscuits.
And then, just to be on the safe side,
he got some bread and some apples
and a basket to carry them in.
"What are you doing?" asked Tumble.

"I thought," said Squeak,
"I might have a picnic."

Squeak went back to the door.

He looked out.

"Hmm," he said.

"I'm ready."

Squeak stepped outside.

"That's a pretty flower," he said.

"What a noisy bee."

Squeak walked, one step at a time,

to the tree at the end of the garden.

"Hmm," said Squeak.
  He put down his basket.
"It's not at all cold – and
  it's certainly not rainy."

So he pulled off his
wellington boots,
and his extra socks,
and his mac and his coat,
and his warmest trousers,
and his mittens and his hat,
and he tied Momma's scarf
to Poppa's umbrella
and he hung them
from the tree.

"Good," said Squeak.

He looked at his basket.

"Now it's time for my…"

"P I C N I C !" yelled Tumble.

"I'm glad you've come," said Squeak.

"This was a good idea," said Momma.

"I love picnics!" said Tumble.

"Lucky you brought so many things," said Poppa.

"Hmm," said Squeak. "It's best to be on the safe side."

And everyone agreed that it was.